COLUMBIA PICTURES PRESENTS A RED WAGON AND FRANKLIN/WATERMAN PRODUCTION A FILM BY ROB MINKOFF STARRING: GEENA DAVIS 'STUART LITTLE 2' HUGH LAURIE AND JONATHAN LIPNICKI MUSIC BY ALAN SILVESTRI EXECUTIVE PRODUCERS JEFF FRANKLIN AND STEVE WATERMAN ROB MINKOFF GAIL LYON JASON CLARK BASED UPON CHARACTERS FROM THE BOOK "STUART LITTLE" BY E.B. WHITE STORY BY DOUGLAS WICK AND BRUCE JOEL RUBIN SCREENPLAY BY BRUCE JOEL RUBIN PRODUCED BY LUCY FISHER AND DOUGLAS WICK DIRECTED BY ROB MINKOFF COLUMBIA PICTURES

**StuartLittle.com**

Screenplay by Bruce Joel Rubin
Story by Douglas Wick and Bruce Joel Rubin

Stuart Little 2™: The New Adventures of Stuart Little
™ & © 2002 Columbia Pictures Industries, Inc. All rights reserved.
Adapted by Laura Hunt
HarperCollins®, ☕®, and HarperFestival® are registered trademarks of
HarperCollins Publishers Inc. Printed in U.S.A.
Library of Congress catalog card number: 2001096645
www.harperchildrens.com
Cover design by Max Maslansky
Interior design by Tom Starace

10 9 8 7 6 5 4 3 2 1
❖
First Edition

# The New Adventures of Stuart Little

Adapted by *Laura Hunt*
Unit photography by *Peter Iovino*
*CG imagery by*
*Sony Pictures Imageworks*

**HarperFestival**®
*A Division of* HarperCollins*Publishers*

# CHAPTER

# 1

## *Too Peewee?*

Stuart Little was happy. Today was the first peewee soccer game of the season. At practice, Stuart had only sat on the bench, but he was sure he could make a difference. True, he was the smallest player on the team. In fact, he was the only mouse on the team, but if the coach would just give him a chance, Stuart could help his team win.

Stuart winced as he watched his older brother, George. Although he tried his best, George couldn't run as fast as the other players.

Stuart and George's parents sat in the stands.

"Every kid has had a chance to play except for Stuart," said Mr. Little.

"Well, there's plenty of time," said Mrs. Little cheerfully. In her arms was their new baby, Martha.

Mr. Little looked at her. "Plenty of time? There are forty seconds left!" he said.

"All right, I admit it," said Mrs. Little. "I'm glad he's not in the game. I don't want him to get hurt."

"Honey, it's peewee soccer," said Mr. Little. "Nobody gets hurt."

At that moment, a boy howled in pain after being kicked in the stomach. As he limped off the field, the coach looked over at the bench to see who he could put in the game. Only Stuart was left.

The coach waved Stuart into the game.

"I won't let you down, Coach," said Stuart as he ran up. The coach gave him a weak smile. The referee blew his whistle.

The ball flew into the air and bounced back-and-forth as the boys kicked it. Stuart was nearly run over when the pack of boys rushed by him.

Suddenly, the ball popped up into the air in the direction of the goal. George and Stuart, who were lagging behind the other boys, found themselves closest to it. They both started running as fast as they could toward the ball. George reached it first.

Wallace, the team bully, yelled at George to kick the ball into the goal! "Kick it, dummy!" said Wallace.

George was scared, but he knew what to do. He took a deep breath, closed his eyes, and kicked the ball at exactly the same time Stuart reached it.

The ball flew into the air with Stuart hanging on, then it ricocheted off Wallace's face. The ball landed in the net. George scored the winning goal! A mob of happy teammates picked up George and carried him off the field.

Mr. and Mrs. Little ran down to the field to look for Stuart. They found him dangling upside-down in the goal netting.

*Do I get an assist?* Stuart thought hopefully.

That night, Stuart and George talked, as they often did, before going to sleep.

"I'm worried that Mom's not going to let me play soccer anymore," said Stuart.

"She wouldn't do that," replied George sleepily.

"She already didn't let me go out for fencing or wrestling or roller hockey," said Stuart.

"What does she want you to do?" asked George.

"Painting or dancing," answered Stuart with a sigh.

"It's hard to get hurt doing those things," said George. "I guess it's my fault for kicking you into the goal."

"That's okay. You won the game. That's the main thing," said Stuart.

"No, the main thing was I hit Wallace in the face," said George, and they both laughed.

# Mouse Overhead

The next day Stuart and George put the finishing touches on a model airplane. George attached the propeller while Stuart sat in the cockpit pretending to fly.

"Wouldn't it be cool if I actually flew this thing?" said Stuart.

"Yeah," George said, rolling his eyes. "Mom's going to let you fly a plane."

Just then, George's friend Will arrived. Stuart was disappointed when George left to play with his friend, leaving Stuart to finish the plane by himself. As Stuart reached under the dashboard, his sweater caught on a switch. Suddenly, the motor roared to life. The plane began taxiing down the dining-room table.

George and Will ran into the room.

"What are you doing?" George yelled over the noise of the engine.

"I'm not doing anything!" screamed Stuart as the plane lifted off the table. George and Will ducked when the plane swooped over their heads. Then it headed for Snowbell the family cat, who dashed into the kitchen.

Mr. Little came into the room and watched in horror as his son tried to gain control of the plane.

Just then, Mrs. Little opened the front door. The plane seemed to have a mind of its own and

flew through the doorway, taking some of the roses in Mrs. Little's hand with it. The frantic Little family followed the plane across the street into Central Park.

Stuart brushed away the rose petals from his eyes. A group of nuns were directly in his path. Stuart quickly turned the plane to avoid hitting the nuns. Then he covered his eyes and screamed as the plane crashed into a thick bush.

The Little family rushed toward Stuart as he crawled out of the wreckage. The wings were dangling off the sides of the plane.

Mr. and Mrs. Little were relieved to find Stuart unharmed.

George was furious when he saw the plane. "You destroyed our airplane!" he shouted.

"With a little glue, we can fix it," said Mr. Little confidently.

"No, you won't!" said Mrs. Little sternly. "That plane is going into the trash. It's much too dangerous."

George threw the plane and manual into a trash can. He left in a huff. Stuart sadly watched him leave.

"Stuart could easily have been killed," Mrs. Little continued. "Painting or dancing. Those are his choices. And I'm no longer too sure about dancing. You don't know what can happen."

After Mrs. Little left, Stuart turned to his father and said, "Mom treats me like a baby."

"She just loves you so much. It's hard for her to think of you in danger," said Mr. Little.

"This has been a bad day," said Stuart with a sigh.

"It's not one of our best days, but it's not that bad," said Mr. Little cheerily. "The thing about being a Little is you always see the bright side. Every cloud has a silver lining."

## *To the Rescue!*

The next day, Stuart slowly drove home from school in his red roadster. Suddenly, a loud squawk filled the air. Then Stuart saw what appeared to be a wounded bird fall out of the sky. *Plunk!* The bird landed right in the passenger seat of his car!

Stuart stopped the car and looked at her. She was an odd bird. On her head she wore goggles and a pilot's helmet. On her shoulders was a scarf.

When Stuart realized she was injured, he raced down the sidewalk. "Out of the way, please! Injured bird coming through!" he shouted.

The bird woke up with a start. "What's going on?" she asked. "Where's Falcon?"

Stuart didn't like the sound of that. At that moment, a terrifying bird swooped down from the sky. Through the windshield, pointed talons and a sharp beak rushed straight at Stuart.

"Drive! Get out of here!" the yellow bird yelled to Stuart, who barely avoided the dangerous attack.

"Get lost, you disgusting vulture!" the bird shouted while waving her wing at the falcon.

"Do we really want to antagonize him?" asked Stuart as he navigated the car through a crowd of people. In front of him, a pizza truck was coming to a stop.

"Uh-oh, we've got a problem," said Stuart.

"You can make it!" said the bird.

The car drove under the truck, narrowly

avoiding being crushed by the tires. But Falcon was still in pursuit.

Stuart saw some long plastic pipes. The perfect hiding place! Stuart zoomed into one of the pipes and screeched to a halt. The falcon landed on the ground and looked around, but he couldn't find the car. He finally gave up and left.

"You did it!" exclaimed the bird.

"Yeah! I did," replied an amazed Stuart.

"So who do I have to thank?" the little bird asked.

"Oh," said the excited mouse. "Forgive me.

My name's Stuart—Stuart Little."

The little bird smiled back and said, "I'm Margalo—just Margalo."

*Margalo*, thought Stuart. *What a great name.*

Stuart brought Margalo home and made her comfortable in the Littles' kitchen. Margalo held out her wing as Stuart wrapped it. It was then that she noticed that Falcon had broken her stickpin. The pin was one of her dearest possessions.

Stuart explained how he came to live with the Little family. He told her about how Mr. and Mrs. Little found him in an orphanage and adopted him. He had a big brother, George, and a brand-new sister, Martha. Stuart was now the middle Little.

Snowbell came into the kitchen for a drink of water. Seeing Margalo, Snowbell jumped back and screamed.

"Hey, Snowbell, meet Margalo," said Stuart excitedly. "She's going to be staying with us for a while."

Snowbell was indignant. "Staying? Are you

out of your mind?" said Snowbell. "She's filthy! She could have germs! How do you know she's not a vagrant or a thief? Get rid of her!"

Just then, Mrs. Little walked through the front door.

"You're in for it now, Missy," Snowbell told Margalo. "Mrs. Little hates when stray animals walk in here off the street. When she sees this, she's going to throw a fit."

Mrs. Little walked into the room and stopped at the sight of Margalo. She picked up

the bird and made kissing sounds. "Such a pretty little birdie," she cooed.

Snowbell shook his head in disgust. "I don't understand," he said. "If I live to be eight, I will never understand."

# *A New Friend*

The Little family welcomed Margalo with open arms. That evening they presented her with a special gift: a jewelry box. In it was a tiny bed covered in a pink-and-white striped bedspread. Next to the bed was a table covered in white lace. It was the perfect home for a little bird.

Margalo's eyes filled with tears. She wiped them and told the Littles that it was the nicest thing anybody had ever done for her. Then she asked where Mrs. Little would keep her jewelry.

"Oh, don't worry about that," said Mrs. Little. "The only thing I really value is my engagement ring."

"Wow, that's beautiful," said Margalo as she looked closely at the ring.

"It's very special to me," said Mrs. Little.

"But now where will you keep it?" asked Margalo eagerly.

"I never take it off except to do the dishes," said Mrs. Little.

The next day, when the house was empty, Margalo removed her bandage and flew to the roof of the Littles' house. She breathed in the fresh air, but she didn't see Falcon soaring high above her. He spotted Margalo and then swooped down straight toward her. He moved closer and closer and closer until . . . he landed right beside her!

Margalo jumped. "Falcon!" she said, startled. "You scared me."

"What can I say? I'm a scary guy," said Falcon. "So Margalo, what's going on here? You cased the joint? Any valuables? Come on . . . thrill me . . . chill me."

"They ain't got much. The mom's got a ring, but its only two carats," replied Margalo.

"Hey! Two carats would feed us for a year," answered Falcon with a wicked grin.

"But Mrs. Little never takes it off . . . " stammered Margalo. "Why don't we just try somewhere else?"

"No. You're set up here. They trust you. They like you," said Falcon. He was beginning to see that Margalo was stalling.

"Remember," said Falcon with a threatening voice, "you're here on business. You're not here to play around. Get me that ring!" With that, he turned and flew away.

Margalo couldn't bring herself to steal the ring from the Littles. They had been so kind to her. Mr. Little built her a birdbath. Mrs. Little added a rug, a swing, and some bird toys to Margalo's jewelry box. But it was Stuart who was the sweetest Little of all. He repaired her

stickpin and surprised her with it. Margalo felt like she belonged to the family.

They did fun things together—as a family—baseball games, barbecues, things she had never done before.

Margalo knew she couldn't wait any longer. Falcon wanted that ring and would do almost anything to get it. She was afraid for the Littles' safety—especially for Stuart's. Margalo knew she didn't have a choice. She had to steal the ring, and fast.

## *Down the Drain*

That evening Margalo had her chance. Before washing the dishes, Mrs. Little took off her ring. When she returned to the kitchen after being called away to change the baby's diaper, she found her ring was gone. She looked around and shouted for help. The family came running.

"It could have gone down the drain!" Mrs. Little said. She left in a hurry to call the plumber.

Stuart peered into the dark drain. Suddenly, he had an idea. Margalo was always saying that life was one big adventure. If Stuart went down the drain to look for the ring, he could have his very own adventure.

Mr. Little wasn't happy about the idea, but he finally agreed. He lowered Stuart down the drain on a string.

After a few minutes, Stuart called up to his father. "There's a lot of slimy stuff on the walls," he said. "I see everything we ate for dinner last week. The pipe just seems to go on and on and on."

Just then, Mrs. Little walked in. "What's on the other end of that string?" she asked with a frown.

"Now, don't get excited," said Mr. Little. "Someone you and I love has volunteered

to go down the drain to look for your ring."

"Stuart? You sent our son down the kitchen drain?" she asked.

"Eleanor, there's no reason to be upset," said Mr. Little calmly as he started to pull up the string. "If there's any problem down there, I will simply pull up the string and . . ." He brought up the string, but Stuart was not on the end of it. The string had broken.

"Now you can get upset," said Mr. Little.

Stuart was splashing around in the water. He told them to hurry. Frantically, his family looked for more string, but there was none to be found.

At that moment, Margalo, who had been watching them through the window, flew in. She unlatched Mrs. Little's pearl necklace from around her neck and lowered it into the drain.

"I got it!" yelled Stuart. Margalo flew straight up, raising both the necklace and Stuart. He was empty-handed but unharmed.

Mrs. Little grabbed Stuart and pressed him against her cheek. "Oh, Stuart," she said. "To think I could have lost you for a stupid ring."

She turned to Margalo and said, "What a wonderful little bird. This family owes you so much."

"You're the best friend I ever had," Stuart added.

Margalo just bowed her head and turned away. She felt terrible about stealing Mrs. Little's ring.

# 6

## *Cat and Mouse*

The next morning when Stuart woke up, he found Margalo was gone. She had left him a present on his pillow: her stickpin. Stuart knew something was wrong. She would never leave without saying good-bye to him.

Stuart decided to leave and look for Margalo that night. First, he asked for George's help.

George agreed to think up a cover story that would explain why Stuart was gone. Next, Stuart packed a few things and tiptoed downstairs as the rest of the house slept.

"Snowbell!" he yelled into the sleeping cat's ear. Snowbell woke up with a start.

"This better be important," Snowbell said gruffly.

"Margalo's missing," said Stuart. "I think the falcon got her."

"I should have been more specific. I meant important to me," replied Snowbell, turning over.

"I'm going out to look for her. I was hoping you'd come with me," said Stuart.

"Why would I do that?" asked the cat sleepily.

"Because we're friends," said Stuart. "And because I'd do the same for you, and because if you don't and the Littles ask where I've gone, George is going to tell them you ate me."

"What? You know something?" he said huffily. "Everybody thinks you're so nice. You're not so nice."

The pair headed outside where it was still dark. Stuart drove the roadster and Snowbell ran along beside him. After a few blocks, the car broke down.

"Well, we gave it our best shot," said Snowbell cheerfully. "Let's go home. Race you for the warm spot under the window."

"We're not giving up," said Stuart. Just then, he noticed a couple of squirrels. "Excuse me," he said. "We're looking for a bird . . . Falcon."

At the mention of Falcon's name, the squirrels screeched and ran away.

"That wasn't very encouraging," muttered Snowbell.

That evening, Stuart and Snowbell decided to get the help of someone who really knew the streets. They waited by the back door of a Chinese restaurant. Inside, there was a loud noise. Suddenly, a striped cat was thrown through the doorway. A man screamed at him then went back inside.

The cat, Monty, gathered himself before jumping back in fright when he saw Snowbell and Stuart. The last time they had met, Snowbell had thrown Monty into the lake in Central Park.

"Snowbell!" said Monty. "Now look, I don't want any more trouble from you."

"Relax, Monty," said Snowbell. "I'm not mad at you anymore."

Monty looked over at Stuart. "Are you still friends with the mouse, or can I eat him?" Monty asked.

"No, you can't eat him," said Snowbell impatiently. "Now pay attention. Do you know where we can find a bird named Falcon?"

"Find him?" said Monty with a shudder. "You don't want to find him. He'd eat you so fast you'd be a pile of falcon poop before you could yell for help."

Snowbell froze in terror.

Stuart could see that Snowbell was losing his nerve. "We're not giving up," said Stuart.

"All right then. It's your funeral," said Monty. "Falcon lives across the park at the tip-top of the Pishkin Building."

*Going Up!*

The next morning, Stuart and Snowbell found the Pishkin Building. They also found a pay phone nearby. Stuart climbed high onto Snowbell's head so he could reach the phone and dialed home. George answered the phone.

"Stuart!" said George.

"Look, I only have a second," said Stuart hurriedly. "I just want you to know that I found Margalo. I'm going off to get her right now, and with any luck, we'll be home by four o'clock."

"But where are you?" asked George.

"Now listen carefully, this is very important. We're at the Pishkin Building—" started Stuart when all of a sudden, an operator came on the line.

"Please deposit thirty-five cents for the next three minutes," said the operator.

"Snowbell, I need more change!" said Stuart.

"Gee, let me just check my pockets," replied Snowbell sarcastically.

The line was cut off.

"Stuart, Stuart! Are you still there?" screamed George, but Stuart was gone.

Stuart and Snowbell dashed across the street. They stood outside the Pishkin Building.

"What are you planning to do, Mighty Mouse?" Snowbell asked Stuart. "Scale the wall?"

"I'll think of something," said Stuart. He noticed a man standing nearby selling helium balloons. Suddenly, Stuart had an idea. He would make his very own hot-air balloon and float to the top of the building!

Brave Stuart made it up to the rooftop. He jumped out and looked around. The area was empty. He took out his homemade bow and arrow and crept around in the shadows.

When Margalo appeared, Stuart was over-joyed. "Margalo!" he said. "I'm here to rescue you!"

"Stuart, I can't go," said Margalo unhappily. "There's something you don't understand. I . . ."

"Maybe I can explain," said Falcon, who suddenly loomed over them.

Falcon led Stuart into his lair where he kept his treasures. He showed Stuart the jewelry that Margalo had stolen for him. In Falcon's claw was Mrs. Little's ring. Stuart was shocked.

"She just pretended to be injured so you'd

take her in," said Falcon with a sneer. "That's what she does."

Stuart was heartbroken. Margalo looked down in shame.

"His little mouse heart is broken," said Falcon with a nasty laugh. He took a few men-

acing steps toward Stuart. "By the way, have you ever had mouse heart? It's delicious."

Stuart jumped back and pointed his bow and arrow at Falcon.

"All right, birdbrain! Give me back that ring," said Stuart. Falcon kept coming. Stuart fired an arrow. Falcon turned sideways and caught it in his mouth. Then he spat it back at Stuart, pinning him to the wall by his collar. Stuart's feet dangled off the ground.

"I hope I wasn't out of line with that bird-brain remark," Stuart said nervously.

Falcon pulled the arrow from out of the wall, and Stuart dropped to the ground. Falcon picked him up and flew to the edge of the building.

"Falcon! Don't!" begged Margalo, but Falcon pushed her away.

"Leave her alone, you overstuffed bully!" shouted Stuart as he struggled with Falcon.

"Wait!" shouted Margalo. "You don't have to kill him!"

"You're right," said Falcon. "The sidewalk will do it."

Falcon dropped Stuart over the building's edge. Stuart desperately grabbed for the side of the building, but he couldn't hold on. He started falling through the air.

Margalo rushed to help, but Falcon kept her away.

# *Going Down!*

**S**tuart screamed as he tumbled through the air. The ground was getting closer and closer. Suddenly, he landed—*plunk*—on a garbage truck. Then garbage landed on top of him. Stuart passed out.

Later, he woke up with a start. He didn't know where he was. Stuart climbed to the top of a pile of garbage to look around. His heart sank. He was on a garbage barge heading out to sea. Manhattan was getting further and further away.

"This is terrible," cried Stuart. "I just want to go home. I know a Little is supposed to always see a silver lining. Maybe this means I'm not really a Little. Maybe I'm just Stuart . . . Nobody."

Stuart began to cry. He reached into his backpack for a hanky and Margalo's stickpin fell

out. Stuart picked up the pin and began to think about his friend.

"There is no silver lining," said Stuart. He stood up and threw Margalo's pin as far as he could into the garbage pile.

"Oh, no, what have I done," cried Stuart, immediately feeling guilty. He quickly scrambled over the garbage to search for the pin. Luckily, he saw it right away. He also saw something else familiar.

"My airplane! I don't believe it! It can't be!" Stuart shouted happily.

Stuart pulled the pieces of the plane out of the rubble. The wings were broken and the front window was smashed.

Stuart looked up at the sky. The sun shone through a gathering of dark clouds. Stuart started smiling.

"The silver lining! This is it!" he cried out. His father always said that every cloud has a silver lining, and Stuart had found his today!

Stuart reassembled the plane using odds and ends from the garbage. Then he hopped into the plane and started taxiing down a runway made from cardboard. The plane went faster and faster but didn't lift off.

"Come on!" said Stuart. "I know you can make it!"

Just as the plane approached the edge of

the barge, it rose into the air. The plane took a dip toward the water, but Stuart pulled it up into the sky. He steered the plane toward Manhattan.

## *Cat and Bird*

George was in big trouble. He had never seen his parents so angry. Before he left to find Margalo, Stuart had asked George to come up with a cover story. Stuart didn't want his parents to worry about him while he was gone, so George told them that Stuart was away rehearsing a new play and sleeping over Will's house. The problem was Mrs. Little missed Stuart so much that she kept asking George questions. And the more questions she asked, the more mixed up his story got. Finally, Mrs. Little went to Will's house to see Stuart. It was then that she discovered that he had never been there at all. Boy, was she mad at George!

George sat in the backseat of a taxi as the Little family looked for Stuart.

"You're in big trouble," said Mr. Little to

George. "For all we know, Stuart could be lying out there, face down, with his . . . "

Mrs. Little gasped.

"Or he could be fine," said Mr. Little quickly. "We don't have to assume the worst. That's not the Little way."

"Oh, Frederick, you're right!" said Mrs. Little cheerfully. "He could be puttering home right now in his shiny, little car."

"Smiling and happy," added Mr. Little dreamily.

"His little whiskers fluttering in the breeze," said Mrs. Little.

"Mom," said George. "I don't think he's put-tering home." He pointed to Stuart's car parked near a building. It had been spray painted and stripped.

"Who would do this?" asked Mrs. Little.

"Tiny, little vandals," replied Mr. Little. The family hurried on its way.

Meanwhile, Snowbell looked up at the towering Pishkin Building. He decided to sneak on an elevator and go to the very top. As the elevator went up, the people standing around him sniffed the air and scowled. At the next floor, everyone rushed off, leaving Snowbell behind.

"Hey, I'm sorry!" he said. "You sleep in the street and see how you smell!"

Snowbell stepped out of the elevator onto the rooftop. All he wanted was to go home and forget the last two days. But first, he had to make sure Stuart was all right. He didn't find Stuart, but he did come across Margalo. She was curled up in a corner looking miserable.

"Where's Stuart?" Snowbell demanded.

Margalo hung her head and said sadly, "He's dead. Falcon killed him."

Snowbell was shocked. "Stuart is dead? He can't be. He's my friend," said Snowbell. He began to cry.

Then Snowbell got angry. "That miserable Falcon! From this day forward, I vow revenge," he shouted. "If that Falcon were here right now, I'd rip his throat out. I'd scratch his face off!"

Margalo pointed above. "That's him," she whispered.

Snowbell squealed in fright. "I'm going to be Falcon poop!" he said as he ran and hid in a paint can.

Falcon landed on the roof and looked around. He spotted Snowbell's tail sticking out of the can. He sneered then kicked the can until it reached the edge of the rooftop. The can teetered on the edge and stopped.

"Snowbell, get out!" Margalo shouted desperately.

Falcon was just about to push Snowbell over the edge when Margalo shouted, "No, don't do it, Falcon . . . or else you'll lose this."

Margalo held up Mrs. Little's beautiful diamond ring.

"I'm through doing what you tell me to do," said the brave little bird. "I'm leaving you, Falcon. Forever!"

Just then, Margalo flew off with the ring.

Falcon followed Margalo as she flew into the air. Just as he was about to grasp her in his claws, Stuart's plane appeared.

## *Mouse and Bird*

"**S**tuart?! You're alive!!" gasped Margalo.

"So far!" replied Stuart. Falcon was coming straight toward him at full speed!

Stuart quickly grabbed the plane's controls. Suddenly, the plane flip-flopped into a backward somersault and tumbled rapidly toward the street below.

Meanwhile on the roof, Snowbell was frantically trying to escape. He only had one problem—the paint can was stuck on his head!

"Careful, now . . . one step at a time," said the frightened cat. But Snowbell took one step too many and plummeted over the edge. Snowbell screamed as the can fell through the air. Suddenly, the handle caught on the end of a flagpole. The can spun around and then stopped.

"I'm alive! I'm alive," he shouted.

Just then, Snowbell saw Stuart's plane approaching in the distance.

At the last moment, Stuart swerved his plane to avoid the can. Just as Snowbell breathed a sigh of relief, Falcon slammed into the can. The can slipped off the pole and fell into the street below.

A cab screeched to a halt in front of the paint can. The Littles jumped out of the cab.

"Stuart!" yelled George as he pointed to Falcon. "Look at that bird. He's bigger than me!"

"When did Stuart learn to fly?" asked Mrs.

Little nervously. Stuart's plane turned upside-down, and Stuart nearly fell out.

"He didn't," said George.

"We've got to save him!" yelled Mr. Little as they jumped back into the cab.

The cab sped away and headed for the entrance to Central Park.

"Come back!" yelled Snowbell.

Meanwhile, even though Stuart and Margalo were flying as fast as they could, Falcon was get-

ting closer and closer. The pair headed into Central Park and then dove into a crowd of people. Stuart skillfully steered the plane around everyone. But Falcon was getting closer still! Stuart took a big chance. He flew down and squeezed through some boxes under a popcorn machine. Falcon was confused by the fancy maneuver and crashed right into the popcorn machine. Glass shattered and popcorn kernels exploded everywhere. Stuart and Margalo escaped in the confusion—but not for long.

Falcon recovered and soon caught up with Stuart and Margalo. He surprised them by sneaking up from behind and grabbing in his talons the wings of Stuart's plane.

Falcon took the plane higher and higher into the sky. Then he grabbed the plane and ripped off the top set of wings. The plane began to spiral down toward the ground. Terrified, Stuart closed his eyes as the ground got closer and closer. But then, miraculously, he heard his name being called. He opened his eyes to see his family below yelling up to him. Stuart snapped out of his daze and pulled up on the controls. The

plane shot back up into the sky.

Stuart suddenly got an idea: Just maybe he could get rid of Falcon once and for all.

Stuart looked behind him and saw that Falcon was flying straight at him. Stuart turned his plane around and pointed it directly at Falcon.

On the ground below, Mrs. Little said in disbelief, "Frederick! What's he doing?"

In horror, Mr. Little cried out, "No, Stuart! Turn! Run away!"

Falcon and Stuart flew toward each other

faster and faster. As he picked up speed, Falcon spread his wings and screeched at the top of his lungs. The terrifying bird filled the entire window of Stuart's plane. Just as the plane and Falcon were about to crash, Stuart pulled out his mother's ring. The diamond reflected sunlight right into Falcon's face. He was temporarily blinded!

"Bye-bye, birdbrain," said Stuart. Then he fell through the plane's escape hatch with his mother's ring in his arms.

Stuart quickly made a makeshift parachute and gently floated toward the ground. Falcon watched Stuart fall then looked up just as the plane collided into him. There was a big crash. Falcon tumbled out of the sky and plummeted to the ground. He was never heard from again.

Unfortunately, the plane crashed into Stuart's parachute and ripped it! Stuart began to fall toward the ground—fast!

Margalo swooped down to rescue Stuart as he fell through the sky. She grabbed Mrs. Little's ring in her claws. Stuart dangled in the air below it. Margalo flapped her wings as fast as she could. They made a safe landing.

The Littles rushed to Stuart and Margalo. Mrs. Little kissed Stuart over and over.

"Stuart, are you all right?" asked Mr. and Mrs. Little at the same time.

"I think so," said Stuart.

"You almost gave me a heart attack!" said Mrs. Little.

"I'm sorry, Mom" said Stuart.

"I'm sorry, too, for not realizing what an amazing, extraordinary little guy you are," Mrs. Little said.

Stuart smiled.

"And one more thing," said Mrs. Little. "If you ever sneak off again without telling me and do something this dangerous, I will lock you in your room until feathers grow out of your nose."

"Yes, Mom," said Stuart as they hugged.

Margalo returned the ring to Mrs. Little, who kissed her on the head. Margalo cooed happily. When Snowbell appeared, the family was all together again. They headed home.

# CHAPTER
# 11

## *Saying Good-Bye*

Later, Stuart and Margalo were kicking around a ping-pong ball like a soccer ball in the Littles' backyard.

"You know, Margalo, I may never work out as a soccer player," said Stuart as he tried to keep the ball in the air. "The ball's so big; my feet are so small. But I've been thinking coaching could really be my thing."

A leaf floated down and landed between the friends. Margalo watched as a flock of birds flew overhead.

"You've always dreamed of going south, haven't you?" asked Stuart.

"Yes," said Margalo. "And every year I'd just watch all the other birds go. The ones who were free."

"You're free," said Stuart softly.

"If I go, we'd be so far apart," said Margalo sadly.

"It wouldn't change a thing," said Stuart bravely.

Later that night, the family gathered on the terrace as the sun was setting.

Margalo looked at each of the Littles who

had gathered around her. She would miss all of them dearly, especially Stuart. But she knew that it was time to go.

"I guess you've been waiting for this a long time," said Mrs. Little.

"All my life," said Margalo. "Only now it's not just talk. It's the real thing."

"Are you scared?" asked George.

Margalo nodded. "The world's pretty big, and I'm pretty small," she said.

"The way I see it, you're as big as you feel," said Stuart. "Just spread your wings and soar."

"I'll miss you, Stuart," said Margalo as they hugged.

"I'll miss you, too," said Stuart.

"I'll miss all of you," said Margalo tearfully.

Margalo turned, lowered her goggles, and flew off. The Littles watched her fly over the park.

"What's the silver lining this time?" Mr. Little wondered out loud.

"She'll be back in the spring," said Stuart.

Stuart smiled as he and his family watched Margalo disappear.